PUFFIN BOOKS

The SMELLIEST Day at the Zoo

Alan Rusbridger lives in London with a family that includes a wife, two daughters, a dog called Angus and a cat called Retro. He has forgotten why the cat is called Retro. He also edits the *Guardian*.

Books by Alan Rusbridger

THE COLDEST DAY IN THE ZOO

THE SMELLIEST DAY AT THE ZOO

THE WILDEST DAY AT THE ZOO

ALAN RUSBRIDGER

The SMELLIEST Day at the Zoo

Illustrated by Ben Cort

PUFFIN

PUFFIN BOOKS

Published by the Penguin Group
Penguin Books Ltd, 80 Strand, London WC2R 0RL, England
Penguin Group (USA) Inc., 375 Hudson Street, New York, New York 10014, USA
Penguin Group (Canada), 90 Eglinton Avenue East, Suite 700, Toronto, Ontario,
Canada M4P 2Y3 (a division of Pearson Penguin Canada Inc.)
Penguin Ireland, 25 St Stephen's Green, Dublin 2, Ireland (a division of
Penguin Books Ltd)
Penguin Group (Australia), 250 Camberwell Road, Camberwell,
Victoria 3124, Australia (a division of Pearson Australia Group Pty Ltd)
Penguin Books India Pvt Ltd, 11 Community Centre, Panchsheel Park,
New Delhi – 110 017, India
Penguin Group (NZ), 67 Apollo Drive, Mairangi Bay,
Auckland 1310, New Zealand (a division of Pearson New Zealand Ltd)
Penguin Books (South Africa) (Pty) Ltd, 24 Sturdee Avenue,
Rosebank, Johannesburg 2196, South Africa

Penguin Books Ltd, Registered Offices: 80 Strand, London WC2R 0RL, England

penguin.com

Published 2006
1

Text copyright © Alan Rusbridger, 2006
Illustrations copyright © Ben Cort, 2006
All rights reserved

The moral right of the author and illustrator has been asserted

Set in Bembo
Made and printed in England by Clays Ltd, St Ives plc

British Library Cataloguing in Publication Data
A CIP catalogue record for this book is available from the British Library

ISBN: 978–0–141–32068–7

To Carl and Ella

Chapter One

It was slap bang in the middle of the hottest day of the year that the drains collapsed outside Melton Meadow Zoo. The first that Mr Pickles, the head keeper, knew of the problem was when Sergeant Saddle, from Melton Meadow Police Station, puffed into his office. He had cycled all the way from the town centre and needed to sit down.

'The bus,' he wheezed. 'It just disappeared.'

'What bus?' asked Mr Pickles, rather concerned about the fact that Sergeant Saddle seemed to have gone mad. 'How can a bus disappear?'

'Down the hole,' gasped Sergeant Saddle. 'A giant hole in the road. In Copp . . . Copplethorpe Road. It ate the bus up. Look for yourself.'

Mr Pickles went to his window and looked over the wall of the zoo. Sure enough, there was the tail end of the Number Seventeen bus in the air, with its front swallowed up by a gaping crater in the ground.

'It landed right on those old drains,' said Sergeant Saddle, mopping his brow, 'so we'll have to close them.'

'Close the drains?' asked Mr Pickles.

'Exactly. No one can use the drains until they're fixed,' said Sergeant Saddle firmly. 'Which might be quite a few days. Any problems, give me a call.'

And with that he disappeared.

The full significance of what Sergeant Saddle had said did not sink in for a few minutes. And, when it did, Mr Pickles called a meeting of all the zoo keepers.

'There's a problem with the drains,' Mr Pickles told the gathered keepers gravely. 'A bus has fallen into them, which means that, er, nothing can go down them.'

'Nothing . . .? But what if we need to go to the toilet?' asked Mr Pomfrey, the penguin keeper.

'Yes, well,' said Mr Pickles, wrinkling his nose at the word 'toilet'. His mother had told him it was rude to talk about toilets or lavatories. 'You'll just have to go into Melton Meadow and use the town, er, conveniences.'

'That's all very well. But what

about the animals?' asked Mr Leaf, the lion keeper. 'I can't take my lions into town.'

'What about the poo?' said Mr Chisel, the chimp keeper, who had a reputation for straight talking.

'Yes, there'll be mountains of the stuff!' declared Mrs Crumble, the crocodile keeper, who didn't believe in beating around the bush either.

'Um, yes,' mumbled Mr Pickles, who felt most flustered indeed. He had been particularly brought up never to speak of such things. 'Well, each keeper will just have to look after the thingummies. Keep everything all tidy and shipshape as, um, possible. Anything else?'

The keepers shook their heads and hurried back to their animals. Things had begun to get decidedly whiffy already.

Mr Pickles went for a little lie-down in his office. But not before he had hung a big notice on the main gates:

Chapter Two

Mr Raja opened the door of the Rhino House and frowned. There on the floor was a large, wet, brown pancake, still fresh and steaming.

'Oh dear,' sighed Mr Raja as he

fetched a spade and scooped it all up
into a big red bucket. Normally he
would have got a high-powered hose
and washed the
stuff down
the drains.
But not
today.

He went to wash his hands and prepare the rhino's tea, when suddenly — *SPLAT!* Mr Raja spun round and saw another torrent of brown stuff cascading on to the newly cleaned floor.

The rhino blinked at him. Or was it a wink? Mr Raja wondered if he was doing it on purpose.

Silly me, thought Mr Raja. *I'm getting all hot and bothered.*

And once again he got out his spade.

By now the bucket was nearly full — and Mr Raja knew that there was no way on earth he could get through the rest of the day with just one bucket. On the other hand, he didn't have any more buckets . . .

Mr Raja sat down and scratched his hot and bothered head. In India, where he had grown up as a boy, they

used cow poo for all kinds of things —
including building houses and as a
fuel. They would collect the cow poo,
dry it out, and burn it. But, as he
gazed into the full bucket in front of
him, he couldn't quite imagine how
a) he could possibly
use it for any
DIY tasks, or
b) make a
barbecue
with it.

But then a brainwave struck him. Fertilizer! That was the other thing they used dung for in India. And Melton Meadow Zoo had some extremely colourful flower beds which he felt sure could just do with a little sprinkling of top-grade compost, or whatever gardeners called it.

'Manure!' he shouted cheerfully, slapping the rhino on its bottom. The rhino shook his head sadly. The heat had clearly gone to Mr Raja's head.

Checking no one was looking, Mr Raja picked up his tin teacup, tip-toed out of the Rhino House and lugged the red bucket over to a nearby border of tulips. Holding his nose with his left hand, he dipped the teacup into the brown sludge and neatly tipped a little melting mound of it at the base of a tulip.

Feeling rather pleased with himself, Mr Raja fertilized a second, and then a third. He imagined how impressed Mr Pickles would be when he heard of his clever idea. But then he looked up to see Mr Emblem, the elephant keeper, who seemed to be copying him!

'Ah, same idea I see,' said Mr Emblem, who was carrying a box of

big round balls of elephant dung. 'I've read that elephant poo makes excellent fertilizer.'

And with that he placed a very large elephant dropping on the head of a garden gnome which was sitting in the middle of the tulips. Mr Raja looked at the poor gnome's face in dismay: it disappeared from view entirely as the dark brown dropping slid down over its shoulders and came to rest on its knees.

Chapter Three

Mrs Crumble, the crocodile keeper, came round the corner on the way back to the Crocodile House to find Mr Raja and Mr Emblem arguing over whose poo made better fertilizer

– a rhino's or an elephant's.

How childish, thought Mrs Crumble. *Typical men!*

But when she got back to the Crocodile House and found a trail of little round brown droppings, she had a second thought, which was, *Maybe it's not such a bad idea after all.*

Mr Crumble was a keen gardener, with a particularly fine vegetable patch full of runner beans, lettuces and – his pride and joy – prize cabbages. Or, at least, he used to win prizes for his cabbages. Recently, at a considerable knock to his pride, he had struggled to make second, or even third, place.

Mrs Crumble thought with delight how gigantic her husband's cabbages could be this year if liberally sprinkled with some top-class crocodile manure.

She collected up all the crocodile droppings she could find into a plastic bag.

The crocodile, who had been woken up as each dropping noisily landed in Mrs Crumble's plastic bag, watched her through half-closed eyes and thought grumpily to himself how very strange his keeper was.

Mrs Crumble left the plastic bag at the zoo gate with a big label saying 'Arthur Crumble' on it. And then she went back to the Crocodile House and texted her husband.

HV LEFT PCKGE @ ZOO 4 U. WOT GR8 MAN-UR 4 YR CABBGES!

Mr Crumble was in town when he picked up the text message, so he drove home via the zoo to pick up the plastic bag.

When he got home he pondered his wife's kind message. For years he had struggled to decipher Mrs Crumble's scribbled notes. While his wife had become rather expert at motor mechanics, it is fair to say she often struggled with her spelling. Now he had to descramble her text messages, which were often just as confusing as her notes had been.

However, this one seemed very simple: 'What a great man you are for your cabbages!'

How typical of Mrs Crumble to send such a thoughtful message, knowing of his recent disappointment in the Melton Meadow Flower and Vegetable Show. He peered into the plastic bag.

'Meatballs!' he chuckled to himself. 'My favourite!' And, as soon as he was home, he set about cooking a rich tomato sauce to go with his dinner.

While the sauce was simmering away, Mr Crumble carefully placed the crocodile droppings on a baking

tray and drizzled a little sunflower oil over them, adding a little pepper and salt for good measure. He placed them in the oven and went out to pick an especially tasty-looking cabbage.

Back at the zoo, Mrs Crumble was feeling very pleased with her efforts and was a bit miffed not to have received at least a little thank you back from Mr Crumble. So she texted him again:

GOOD MAN-UR?

This one puzzled Mr Crumble, now back in the kitchen, as he put a knob of butter over his lightly boiled cabbage. They were very fond of each other, but it wasn't like Mrs Crumble to go to the trouble of telling him 'What a good man you are' twice in one day. And why the question mark? He texted back:

GOOD WOMAN-UR

And with that he poured the tomato sauce over the crocodile droppings and sat down to eat.

Back at the zoo, Mrs Crumble frowned. Why was Mr Crumble telling her what a good woman she was?

'I don't know,' she said out loud. 'What's he on about?'

The crocodile shook his big head in

disdain. His keeper seemed to be getting stranger by the minute.

In the meantime, Mr Crumble chewed enthusiastically on his first bite of crocodile poo. It tasted very funny. He tried spooning some more tomato sauce on to his fork, but it still tasted very odd indeed. He didn't wish to hurt his wife's feelings, so he texted once more:

DID UR MUM MAKE T MEATBALLS?

He picked away at some of his delicious cabbage, and thought that perhaps he should be the one to make dinner from now on. His phone peeped and he scrolled down for the response.

WOT MEATBALLS?

Mr Crumble stared at the little brown balls on the plate in front of him, and cut one in half. It seemed to have half-chewed grass inside it. He texted Mrs Crumble:

IN PLSTC BAG?

This time, he didn't try any more meatballs, but waited for the response.

NOT MEATBALLS! MANURE!

Mr Crumble stared in horror at his mobile phone, rooted to his chair as his stomach heaved and rumbled and gurgled. Then he rushed over to the kitchen sink where, I'm afraid to say, he was violently sick.

Back at the zoo, Mrs Crumble couldn't believe her husband was so stupid. She sent him a final text:

WOT A DAFT MAN-UR

'He's eaten your poo!' she screeched at the crocodile.

The crocodile eyed Mrs Crumble sorrowfully. She was obviously stark-raving bonkers. He turned round and decided it might be a good time to go back to sleep.

Chapter Four

Back in his office, Mr Pickles was gazing out of his window, toying with the idea of catching up with the Test Match score. Suddenly – *CRASH!* – the window shattered, showering broken glass all over the office.

'What on earth is − ?' shouted Mr Pickles.

But the question froze on his lips. He could see at a glance what was going on. Half a dozen chimps had broken loose from Mr Chisel, their keeper, and escaped from the Chimp House and were running riot in Mr Pickles's prize flower beds.

It turned out that the flower beds were a much better place to play than the chimp house, which to tell the truth, the chimps had been getting rather bored with lately. They had discovered a number of round balls hidden among the flower beds – too small and hard for football, too big for

cricket. But just perfect for throwing
at each other.

And even better for throwing at the
head zoo keeper.

Mr Pickles ran out of his office, shaking his fist. He felt really quite cross. The chimps, however, thought he was urging them on. Brilliant! Mr Pickles was obviously much more fun than Mr Chisel – maybe they could even swap keepers after this.

One chimp picked up a large ball of elephant dung. *THUD!* It landed on the top of Mr Pickles's head with a painful thump. The chimps screeched with laughter. Mr Pickles was such a sport for joining in the fun.

'I'm so sorry about this,' gasped
Mr Chisel. 'I was just trying to give
them some air while I cleaned their
house.'

Mr Pickles spun round and saw (far too late) another chimp with his foot in the middle of one of Mr Raja's big runny piles of rhino poo. With an elegant flick of his foot, the chimp scooped up the soggy mound and splattered it slap bang in the middle of Mr Pickles's horrified face.

For a few seconds the head keeper of Melton Meadow Zoo stood frozen like a statue. Slowly he opened one eye, then the other – revealing two white holes in an otherwise brown and slippery face. Three or four drops of poo slid off his chin on to

his clean white shirt. A large bluebottle
settled on his nose.

He opened his mouth, spitting out
little flecks of poo from his lips and
teeth and setting off a fresh round of
amused screeches from the chimps.

But no words would come to the head keeper. For the first time in his long life Mr Pickles was speechless.

Glaring through his brown poo mask he retreated to his office, dodging, with varying success, one or two elephant-dung missiles as he went.

Miss Busby, the zoo secretary, managed to suppress a snigger as Mr Pickles dripped into the outer office. 'Shall I run you a bath?'

Chapter Five

The next morning Miss Ingleby, the dung-beetle keeper, received a call from a very flustered-sounding Mr Pickles.

'It's all a disaster!' he declared –

a little overdramatically, Miss Ingleby thought. 'You must come now!'

Miss Ingleby sighed as she put down the phone. She really didn't understand why people couldn't be more like dung beetles. There was never even a whiff of amateur dramatics from her precious insects. Even if there was that constant slight whiff of a different kind.

Miss Ingleby had a sudden thought before leaving for Mr Pickles's office and stopped just for a second to pop something in a matchbox to take with her.

'The neighbours are complaining,'
Mr Pickles announced when Miss
Ingleby arrived.

'I should think the whole town's
complaining,' said Miss Ingleby sharply.

'It's thirty degrees in the shade and the pong is quite awesome.'

'Yes, well. Sergeant Saddle has been round to check up on us because of the complaints – interrupting the Test Match, I might add – and he's not impressed,' said Mr Pickles. 'So what we need is a plan. An emergency plan,' he added decisively.

'Righto,' agreed Miss Ingleby, waiting to hear Mr Pickles's plan. But Mr Pickles didn't appear to have anything else to say. He looked at Miss Ingleby hopefully.

Miss Ingleby sighed for the second

time that morning. 'I was wondering about these,' she said, opening a little box to reveal two small, round, brown insects.

Mr Pickles looked confused.

'Dung beetles!' she said brightly.

'What about dung beetles?' asked Mr Pickles.

'Well, they eat dung,' said Miss Ingleby.

'They eat . . . thingummy?' asked an astonished Mr Pickles. 'How extraordinary. Do they, er, like it?'

'Love it. Breakfast, lunch and supper. Nothing but dung,' said Miss Ingleby. She scrunched up her nose at the little beetles. 'Yum, yum, yummy, eh?'

The dung beetles frowned back. Anyone would think they were children.

'Well, let's set them to work,' said Mr Pickles excitedly. 'I shall ring

Sergeant Saddle and tell him we have an emergency plan.'

He called out to Miss Busby, his secretary, to ring Sergeant Saddle on his mobile phone. Miss Ingleby tipped the beetles out of the little box into a large metal wastepaper bin and then – much to Mr Pickles's horror – produced a large elephant dropping from her rucksack and carefully placed it in the bin.

'There you are,' she cooed to the beetles. 'Lovely num–nums!'

The beetles glowered back.

'Now, how much thingummy can a whatsit beetle eat a day?'

'About fifty grams,' said Miss Ingleby.

'And how many beetles do you have?' asked Mr Pickles.

'One hundred and fifty-two,' said Miss Ingleby. 'When I last looked.'

Mr Pickles got out his calculator and fed in:

152 x 50 = 7,600

'Seven point six kilograms a day!' Mr Pickles was now very excited. 'Just wait until I tell Sergeant Saddle this.'

A sound like a tiny burp echoed around the metal wastepaper bin. Miss Ingleby looked in and saw two beetles, green with indigestion and mopping their brows.

Mr Pickles called through to Miss Busby: 'Have you managed to get Sergeant Saddle yet?'

'Now, remember,' said Mr Pickles to Miss Ingleby, stabbing away at his calculator, 'we have 4,000 animals in the zoo. And that means three tonnes of, um, what-do-you-call-it a day.'

'Right,' said Miss Ingleby, taking the calculator off him and doing some sums of her own. 'That's three tonnes, which is, let me see, 3,000 kilograms, which is, er, 3 million grams.'

'Which means,' groaned Mr Pickles, 'that it would take 395 days for all our dung beetles to eat just one day's worth of poo.'

There was another tiny belch from the tin bin as one of the beetles choked on a stringy bit of dung.

'That's over a year!' said Mr Pickles.

'To eat one day of thingummy.' He slumped back into his armchair in despair.

Just then Miss Busby called in from the outer office, 'I have Sergeant Saddle on the line. Shall I put him through?'

'Oh no,' groaned Mr Pickles. 'Tell him I'm busy.'

Miss Ingleby picked up the metal wastepaper bin – complete with burping beetles and dung – and tiptoed out of the room.

Chapter Six

Half an hour later Miss Ingleby returned with a Second World War gas mask which her grandfather had used as a soldier. She handed it to Mr Pickles and suggested they did a tour of the zoo. She thought it best that they saw how bad – or smelly – things had got.

'Let's go and see if any of the other keepers are doing any better,' she hissed.

Mr Pickles struggled to strap on the gas mask. It was made out of heavy green rubber with two glass portholes to look out of and a long round sticky-out snout where the nose should be.

'Thank–oo,' said Mr Pickles after he had finally stretched it over his head. The gas mask made him sound as if he had a heavy cold and made him look like an alien.

'Shall we go and see how the keepers are getting on?' said Miss Ingleby.

'Goo'... idea,' snuffled Mr Pickles, who was beginning to feel like a Martian.

'I think it might be a good idea to do the smelliest first.'

'Mmmm,' mumbled Mr Pickles, as sweat began to trickle down the inside of his mask.

Miss Ingleby, who was an expert in all types of animals, consulted a list she had drawn up and led Mr Pickles to the porcupines.

They were twenty metres away from the Porcupine House when the smell hit them. Or rather, hit Miss Ingleby. Mr Pickles was struggling for breath a little, but even through his Second World War gas mask he picked up on the unbelievable stench wafting across the grass from the building they were approaching.

'A combination of pee, poo and scent,' said Miss Ingleby briskly, pinching her nose with her left hand.

'Ah,' gurgled Mr Pickles.

'The males pee on the females. They both squirt scent from their bottoms. Glands near their bottoms to be precise. And –'

'Charming,' said Mr Pickles, who had learned quite enough about porcupines for one day.

'Er, well, how about the wolves?' asked Miss Ingleby, leading her boss to the next building.

As they got close they walked into a wall of pong like a cross between a week-old nappy and a month-old rotting fish.

'Phwoooar,' groaned Miss Ingleby, who until now had been a model of composure. 'I think they must be spraying scent around to disguise the smell of all that —'

'Thingummy,' interrupted Mr Pickles.

'Er, yes, thingummy,' agreed Miss Ingleby.

'Shall we move on?' asked Mr Pickles.

'Yes,' said Miss Ingleby quickly, relieved not to have to get any nearer the wolves. 'What about the turkey vultures?'

'If we must,' sighed Mr Pickles, who now felt as if his head was about to burst inside the confounded gas mask.

'I'm afraid these might be very

whiffy indeed,' warned Miss Ingleby. 'Turkey vultures pee and poo on themselves . . .'

'They do WHAT?' shrieked Mr Pickles.

'Pee and poo on themselves,' repeated Miss Ingleby. 'And they also vomit all over other animals if they feel threatened.'

'Ah,' said Mr Pickles.

'Apparently the vomit smells particularly disgusting,' said Miss Ingleby helpfully.

'Er, why don't we give the vultures a miss?' said Mr Pickles, who was now feeling sick, not to mention steaming hot and extremely bothered.

And so it went on. Miss Ingleby started scribbling a list of all the animals they visited.

Hyenas, wrote Miss Ingleby. *Smearing stinky paste all around their cages.*

Skunks, she scribbled. *Saw Mr Pickles coming and squirted him with thick oil spray. Dis . . . GUST . . . ing!*

Dingoes, she wrote next. *Have been rolling in their own poo all morning. Uuuugh!*

Polecats . . . spray revvvvvv-OL--- ting!

Camels . . . burping all the time. Gross.

Cows . . .  *farting all the time. Really gross.*

Mongooses . . .

But before they could manage any more Mr Pickles threw up at Miss Ingleby's feet.

One of the mongooses looked up at the two zoo keepers in disgust. Humans were just BEYOND GROSS.

Chapter Seven

It was now Saturday afternoon and as
Mr Pickles lay in the bath at the zoo
with his yellow rubber duck, trying to
recover from the morning's events, he
realized the crisis had now been

going on for twenty-four hours. Which meant — if Miss Ingleby's figures were correct — that there was now approximately three tonnes of whatsit lying around in his zoo. Three tonnes!

He leaped out of the bath and, as soon as he'd dragged some new clothes on — thoughtfully fetched from his home by Miss Busby — he called a meeting of all the keepers.

While they assembled, he nipped out of the front door of the zoo and walked round to Copplethorpe Road to see how Sergeant Saddle was

getting on with
the stuck bus.

He was greeted
by an extremely
hot and bothered
Sergeant Saddle,
waving his arms at
a giant bulldozer
which was pulling at a
long rope without, it seemed, much
success.

'How are you getting on, Sergeant?'
asked Mr Pickles. 'Only I've got three
tonnes of thingummy still piling up
and, well, it's jolly pongy.'

'What's thingummy?' asked a mystified Sergeant Saddle.

'Whatsit,' said Mr Pickles. 'Whatcha-macallit. Who-jermaflip.'

Sergeant Saddle looked blank.

'Number Twos!' said Mr Pickles, blushing.

'Number Twos,' said Sergeant
Saddle crossly, 'are your problem. My
problem is Number Seventeens. In
other words, getting this 'ere bus out
of this 'ere hole.'

And, with that, he went back to
waving his arms at the bulldozer and

Mr Pickles slunk back to his office, where all the keepers were waiting.

'Now then,' he began briskly, 'I've been talking to Sergeant Saddle, and he's doing his best to pull the bus out of the hole. But that might take a little while, so we just need to sort out our emergency plan. Any ideas?'

Mr Leaf, the lion keeper, spoke up first. 'Why don't we drain the Penguin Pool and put all the poo there?'

Mr Pomfrey, the penguin keeper, was outraged. 'Why pick on the penguins?' he said. 'What's wrong with the Lion House?'

'Why don't we just call the bin men and ask them to take it away?' asked Miss Ingleby.

'Health and safety,' said Mr Pickles gravely. None of the keepers knew what that meant, but it sounded impressive.

'Why don't we bag it up and sell it at the front door?' said Mrs Crumble brightly. 'Top-rate manure at bargain-basement prices! Mr Crumble put it on his vegetables.' She added: 'After he'd finished trying to eat it.'

The other keepers all looked rather disturbed at this revelation. Mind you, they – like the croc – also thought Mrs Crumble was a little strange at times.

'We are a zoo, not a garden centre,' said Mr Pickles severely. 'And anyway, I don't think our neighbours would thank us for lining up hundreds of bags of you-know-what all the way up and down the street.'

The keepers all fell silent.

'Can I make a suggestion?' asked Mr Emblem, the elephant keeper. 'The real problem is outside the zoo, not inside.'

'Very helpful, I'm sure,' said Mr Pickles sarcastically.

'I just meant . . .' said Mr Emblem. 'Well, I just meant, why don't we help pull the bus out of the hole?'

'I suppose you had three Weetabix for breakfast,' said Mr Pomfrey.

'Not me,' said an exasperated Mr Emblem, 'the elephants!'

There was a moment of stunned silence. And then all the other keepers began clapping.

'Brilliant!' said Mr Pickles, looking very relieved. 'Absolutely brilliant!'

'What about the rhinos?' said Mr Raja.

'The more the merrier!' said Mr Pickles.

'What about the chimps?' asked Mr Chisel.

'Not that merry!' said Mr Pickles very firmly.

Chapter Eight

An hour later, Mr Pickles led a slow procession of zoo keepers and very large animals out through Melton Meadow Zoo's main gates as the traffic came to a standstill.

A crowd of neighbours had just begun gathering in the road, with large banners.

One read: **NO MORE SMELLS!**

Another said: **STOP THE PONG!**

And another read:

★

In Copplethorpe Road Sergeant Saddle had taken a brief break from waving at the struggling bulldozer. He sat down in the hot sun, laid his head against a tree and began to daydream.

He imagined himself lying on a lilo in a swimming pool in the Caribbean. The cool water was lapping his feet . . . and he was sipping from a refreshing fruit cocktail . . . Towards him came giant elephants, enormous rhinos and Mr Pickles . . .

Mr Pickles?

Mr Pickles!

There he was – in the flesh, not in a dream – standing right over him, as he struggled to put his helmet back on.

'Ah, Sergeant Saddle,' said Mr Pickles smugly. 'Surprised you can find time for a snooze at a time like this.'

Sergeant Saddle's face – which was always quite red – flushed beetroot with embarrassment.

'It's been a long day,' he muttered. And then, as his eyes began to refocus on the scene around him, he saw to his astonishment that he was

surrounded by elephants and rhinos,
all on long ropes held by chuckling
keepers. 'Wha . . . what are *th–they*
doing here?' he stammered.

'Oh, just thought we might give you a hand,' said Mr Pickles cheerily.

'Well, if they escape . . .'

'They won't escape,' said Mr Pickles. 'Now, where shall we tie the ropes?'

By now a huge crowd had gathered in Copplethorpe Road as the keepers tied their ropes to the disappearing bus and Seargent Saddle directed everyone into position.

When everyone was ready he held his big white hanky in the air and shouted 'PULL!'

The bulldozer roared into life, sending giant balloons of smoke into the air. The bus trembled a little, but wouldn't budge.

'PULL!' shouted Mr Pickles at the top of his voice.

At this signal four elephants and four rhinos began to trudge slowly away from the bus, one deliberate lumbering step at a time. The ropes tightened and groaned.

The bus shuddered. And wobbled. And grated and screeched. And then, inch by inch, it began to emerge from the chasm in Copplethorpe Road.

'PULL!' cried the crowd.

'PULL!' shouted Mr Pickles, who was by now quite hoarse.

'PULL!' shouted Sergeant Saddle, who was feeling a bit left out.

And so it was – after twenty minutes of heaving, shouting, cheering, sweating

and groaning (and that was just Mr
Pickles) — that the Number Seventeen
bus was once again where it should
have been: in the middle of
Copplethorpe Road, rather than
nose-down in a drain.

Mr Pickles beamed at the crowd,
who had broken into applause. He was
gratified to notice a banner held high.
PONG OFF, PICKLES! had been
crossed out and replaced with
PICKLES FOR PRESIDENT!

An hour later the crowd had gone
home, the animals were back in the
zoo, the keepers were busy with their

high-pressure hose pipes and Mr Pickles and Sergeant Saddle were enjoying a well-earned cup of tea together . . . with just an eye on the Test Match in the corner of the room.

And a month later, Mr Crumble won first prize for the biggest cabbage the Melton Meadow Flower and Vegetable Show had ever seen.